Natalie

Wants a Puppy

Other titles in the That's Nat Series

Natalie

Wants a Puppy

Dandi Daley Mackall

ZONDERVAN.com/
AUTHORTRACKER
follow your favorite authors

We want to hear from you. Please send your comments about this book to us in care of zreview@zondervan.com.

For Grace Eberhart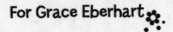

ZONDERKIDZ

Natalie Wants a Puppy
Copyright © 2009 by Dandi Daley Mackall
Illustrations © 2009 by Lys Blakeslee

Requests for information should be addressed to:

Zondervan, Grand Rapids, Michigan 49530

Library of Congress Cataloging-in-Publication Data
Mackall, Dandi Daley.
  Natalie wants a puppy / by Dandi Daley Mackall ; [Lys Blakeslee, illustrator].
p. cm.– (That's Nat!)
        Summary: When six-year-old Natalie learns her parents are adopting a
baby from another country, she is not sure she will like being an older sister and
she would much rather get a puppy.
        ISBN 978-0-310-71571-9 (softcover)
        [1. Adoption–Fiction. 2. Brothers and sisters–Fiction. 3. Family life–Fic-
tion. 4. Christian life–Fiction.] I. Blakeslee, Lys, 1985- ill. II. Title.

        PZ7.M1905Nr 2009
        [Fic]–dc22   2008049739

Editor: Betsy Flikkema
Art direction & design: Merit Kathan

Printed in the United States of America

11 12 13 14 • 22 21 20 19 18 17 16 15 14 13 12 11 10 9 8 7 6 5 4 3

Table of Contents

Chapter 1

Detective Nat

My name is Detective Nat. That's what.
Only you might know me as Natalie 24.
Or Nat 24.
Or Nat.
Or maybe Natalie Elizabeth, if you heard my mom calling me when she was aggravated.

But today I am mostly Detective Nat. On account of there's a mystery going on around here.

"Come on, Percy," I whisper to my white, fluffy cat, who is also my mom and dad's cat. "You can be my helper detective."

Percy prances to my bed and jumps up. Then he curls himself into a white, fluffy ball on my pillow.

I tiptoe out of my bedroom and look both ways down and up the hall. I can hear my mom talking on the phone in the kitchen. I can't hear her words, but she is laughing at the phone.

This is an okay thing. 'Cause I am looking for clues. Clues are like hints that help detectives find out what that mystery is all about. I already have some of those clues.

Mom got a phone call yesterday and screamed her head off ... in a happy way.

She called Daddy, and I heard him scream his head off, all the way through the phone.

When I asked why people were screaming their heads off, Mom said, "We have some good news.

Daddy and I will tell you later. Be patient."

When I asked Daddy why people were screaming their heads off, Daddy said, "We have some good news. Mommy and I will tell you later. Be patient."

Daddy came home with packages and hid them.

One of those packages is in our closet that lives in our hall. And that's the clue I'm going for right now.

If you are also a detective, you maybe thought those packages are Christmas presents. Only you are wrong about that. I have one more week of kindergarten, and then it's summer. And Christmas isn't in summer.

Or, you maybe thought those packages were secret birthday presents for me. But the two and four in my "Natalie 24" name come from my birthday being on Month Number Two and Day Number Four. February four. And that's still a very, very, very, very long ways away. I promise.

And now you get why there's a mystery.

I open the door to our hall closet. Only I can't reach the light switch. But I am a lucky detective anyways. 'Cause that big, flat box Daddy hid in this closet is open. And I'm guessing Mommy peeked at it before me.

I reach inside the box and feel strings in there.

Plus, there are bars holding those strings. I pull as hard as I can. It comes out a little bit. This big stringy bar thing looks like a big, funny cage. We have one of those in kindergarten for Ham the Hamster.

This stringy bar cage is a big, fat clue. Only I don't know why.

From the kitchen comes a very loud laugh from my mom. "No! We haven't told her! We thought we had months yet. I can't even imagine what she'll say."

I think *I'm* the "her" nobody's told yet, and I'm the "she" in "I can't even imagine what she'll say." So I close the hall closet and sneak on tiptoes up to the kitchen door.

Now I can hear everything my mom says.

Mom uses her softer voice. Only I am close enough to hear those soft words. "I don't even know if Nat understands what it means to adopt," she says.

Clue: Adopt.

I *do* kind of know this word. My bestest friend who is a boy, Jason, got a cat from a place called *Adopt-A-Pet*. Only they wouldn't give him another one when that one ran away from home.

"I think she'll be as excited as we are!" Mommy says louder to the phone.

Clue: I will be excited about this mystery.

"Are you kidding?" Mom laughs her head off. "Can you just imagine the kinds of names Nat would come up with?"

Clue: The mystery is something that needs a name.

I am a good namer. I didn't name Percy. But I named all of my stuffed animals myself. Like Brownie. And Blackie. And Whitey. And Bunny, which is my stuffed bunny. Plus also, Steg-O my dinosaur.

"Right!" Mom laughs another head off. "Or Fido or Spot, or—" Only she doesn't finish that one 'cause she's still laughing too much.

And I don't even need her to finish or talk anymore. On account of my head is adding up all of these clues. Like that I will be excited. And that Mom and Dad didn't tell me this surprise yet. And that there is a string cage in our closet. And I know that word *adopt*. And that I am going to name something. Plus, especially this last clue:

I would name this something Fido or Spot.

And guess what! Those are my dog names!

So even if you're not a detective like me, you ought to have this mystery solved by now.

I'm getting a puppy!

Chapter 2

Talk, Talk, Talk ...

"Mom! Mommy!" my mouth yells, and my feet run to the kitchen instead of staying hiding.

"Natalie, please. I'm on the phone," Mom says. "I thought you were taking a nap."

I let her think that so I could be a detective better. "I *need* to talk to you *now*!" I shout. This feels like a true thing. I *have* to tell her I know this secret. I have a gazillion questions about my new puppy.

"Well, you're going to have to wait, Natalie," Mom says. "I'm on the phone with your grandmother."

"Granny won't care!" I know that my granny would want me to know all about my puppy.

3

"Nat, I'm talking to your California grandmother. This is long distance. Please wait until I'm finished."

Regular Granny is my dad's mom. She lives in our same town. My mom is talking to Different Granny, who is my mom's mom. And that can get mixed up in your head.

"Sorry, Mom," my mom says to the phone. "Go ahead. What were you saying?"

I start to tell Mommy why I have to tell her something. But she shakes her head at me. It is really much hard not talking about my puppy. My heart is thumpy. Inside, I am talking about my puppy over and over: *I'm getting a puppy! I'm getting a puppy!*

"She's right here," my mom says to the phone. "Want to talk to her?"

I reach for the phone.

Before she hands it over, Mom whispers to the phone, "Okay, Mom. But don't tell you-know-who about you-know-what. Bill wants to be in on it."

I know that *you-know-who* is me. And *you-know-what* is my puppy. That's what!

I take the phone and shout at it, "Hi, Gran!" California is very much farther away from here than kindergarten is, or even Florida.

"It's okay, Nat," Different Granny says. "I can

hear you loud and clear, honey."

I want to spill out this whole secret that I know. Only my mom is staring at me. And my dad, who goes by the name of Bill, wants to be in on it.

"How's the weather there?" Different Granny asks.

"Okay," I say. I can't say more because that mystery secret might come out with more talking.

"I see." Different Granny isn't saying more either. "Well, you have a good final week in kindergarten, Natalie."

"Okay. Bye!" I shout. I hang up the phone 'cause I *have* to ask my mom about my puppy.

"Natalie, don't hang up!" Mom cries. She grabs the phone. Only it's too late. "I wasn't finished talking to your grandmother." She's already punching in those California numbers.

"But I want to talk to *you*!" I say.

"We will, Nat. I just need to ask Mom something." She frowns at the phone. "Busy?" She punches the numbers again.

"Mommy?" I try.

"Natalie, please go play in your room until your dad gets home." She gives a mean look at the phone again. "Still busy?" She sets the phone on the counter and goes to the fridge.

I watch from the hall, like a detective. Mom

opens the fridge and stares in. Only she doesn't get anything. Then she laughs, even though our fridge isn't so funny. She holds her head and does a little spin. My mom is dancing in our kitchen.

"Yes!" she whisper-shouts. She looks up at our roof. "Thank you, God!"

I really want to ask my mom about my puppy. Only she is acting pretty funny.

Mom whizzes out of the kitchen so fast that she bumps into me. "Oops! Natalie, what are you doing here?"

"I'm—," I begin, thinking I could tell her I'm Detective Nat and know about my puppy.

But she talks too fast. "Listen, Nat. Daddy and I want to have a talk with you tonight."

"You do?" My heart is thumpy again. "Can we do it now?"

"Not until Daddy gets home."

I don't think I can wait that long. "But—"

"Nat, please," Mommy begs. "I have a million things to do. Go play until your dad gets home, okay?"

This is not okay. I can't play. I *have* to talk about my puppy. "Can I call Laurie?" Laurie is my bestest friend who is a girl.

"Sure. Go ahead. Great idea. Call Laurie. But let me know as soon as you hear Daddy, okay?" She rushes off to her bedroom.

I sit on the kitchen stool and call Laurie.

The phone rings two times before someone answers, "Sarah's Tattoo and Bar-B-Q."

I know this is Laurie's house. And this is Brianna, one of Laurie's sisters, the not-too-nice one. Sarah is the nice sister. She wears lipstick, but not tattoos. "Is Laurie home?" I ask.

"Oh, it's you," Brianna says. She always sounds like she wants it to be anybody but me. "Laurie!" she screams. The phone clunks.

Then Laurie comes on. "Hi!"

"Laurie, I solved a mystery!"

"Cool!" Laurie says.

"Plus, it's a secret. Only not. 'Cause I know this secret."

"What, Nat?" Laurie sounds all smiley-faced.

"I'm getting a puppy! That's what!" Those words spurt out of my mouth and into the phone.

"A puppy!" Laurie squeals. "Wow, Nat! That's so cool!"

"I know!" I love that my bestest friend can be excited with me.

"How come now, Nat?" Laurie asks. "It's not even your birthday."

"Or Christmas," I add.

"*I* know!" Laurie says. "I'll bet they're giving you a getting-out-of-kindergarten present!"

I hadn't even thought about that. "I bet you're right. We got our teacher, Miss Hines, a present for making it through kindergarten. She just gets a book. I can't believe I get a puppy."

"What kind of puppy, Nat?" Laurie asks.

"I don't know."

"Didn't you ask?"

"No," I answer. "But I will. When Daddy comes home, they're going to talk to me. And I'll find out everything."

"You are so lucky!" Laurie says.

"And you too. 'Cause you can play with it," I tell her.

"Yeah!"

I hear our front door open. "Laurie, Daddy's home! I have to go and be talked to!"

Chapter 3

Mystery Mistakes

I run very fast to the front door. But my mom beats me to it. She hugs Daddy. And Daddy hugs her, even though he's carrying packages. I run up and share this hug.

"I got everything," he says, holding out his arms. They have shopping bags hanging on them.

"Mom says we get to talk!" I tell him.

Daddy dumps his shopping bags and picks me up. He twirls me around, which he never does inside the house almost. "You bet we'll talk," he says. "Have we got news for you, kiddo!"

I feel kinda grown-up, on account of I also have news for them. Their news for me is "You're getting a puppy!" And my news for them is "I know!"

"Can we have dinner first?" Mom says, laughing.

"No!" I beg. "I can't wait to talk!"

"I'm with Nat on this one," Daddy says.

"Okay," Mom agrees.

I plop down on the floor right where we are, just inside our front door and on our living room rug.

"Can't we at least sit at the table?" Mom asks.

Daddy plops down beside me. "Nope."

Mom laughs and plops down with us. We are three sitting-down-on-the-floor people.

My mom starts the talking. "Nat, I hope you know how happy your dad and I are. We love you, and we're so blessed with this family God's given us. It's because our life is so wonderful, that sometimes we want more family."

"I *know*!" My dog will be a part of our family forever.

"You do, huh?" Daddy says, all smiley-faced. "What do you know?"

"I know the mystery!" I can't hold this in any longer. "I know the big secret. That's what!"

"Natalie!" Mom is big in her eyes. "But how—"

"I heard you. And I found stuff. Like that string cage thing in the closet—"

"That string ... the pen?" Mom says. "The playpen?"

"Yep. And I'm so excited! Like you knew I'd be."

Daddy laughs. "We sure hoped so."

"And I'll think up a great name! Like Foofy. Or Fido. Or … or maybe I'll wait and name it when we see what kind it is."

"What kind?" Mommy asks.

"You mean like a boy or a girl, right?" Daddy says. "I can answer that right now. A boy."

I think about this. I know many good boy names.

"Natalie," Mommy says, "do you understand that we're adopting?"

"I know that word, *adopt*," I tell them. "When can we go pick him out?"

"It doesn't work like that, honey," Daddy says.

"Jason's whole family went to the Adopt-A-Pet. They got to vote on their cat," I explain.

"Well, it's not that easy for us," Mommy says.

"Why not?"

She pushes my hair out of my face. "Because it's a lot easier to adopt a cat, sweetheart."

"But not a puppy?" I don't understand this part.

"A puppy?" Daddy says. He looks fast at Mommy, then back to me. "Nat, what do you think we're talking about here?"

"My puppy!" I shout. On account of this is making my head hurt. "I want to pick out my own puppy!"

Mom and Dad stare at me. Then they look at each other and bust out laughing. They laugh so hard they fall off the floor onto their backs.

"It's not funny!" I shout. "Why can't I pick out my own puppy?"

That makes them laugh all over again.

When they finally stop laughing and sit back up, Mom puts her arm around my shoulder. "Natalie," she says, "we're not getting a puppy. We're getting a baby!"

Chapter 4

The Truth about Babies

"A baby?" I shout. "Are you sure?"

I look at my mom's stomach. She told me babies come from there. "You're not fat like Bethany's mom was fat."

Daddy pats Mommy's tummy. "Hmmm … she's right, you know."

I stare at her stomach. "Plus also, I don't remember seeing anybody else in there when I was there." I think I would have remembered that one.

They laugh their heads off. Only not for too long.

"I'm sorry, Nat," Mom says. "We're not laughing at you. We're just so happy. We've been waiting such a long time. We're adopting a baby from China."

"From China? Like Anna's China?" Anna is in my kindergarten class. She told us all about her grandparents being from China.

"Will it talk American?" I ask.

"Eventually," Mom answers. "We'll count on you to help with that."

I am trying to get used to this idea. A baby in our house? Where will it live? Jason's baby brother lived in Jason's room. And all it did was cry. Plus, it was wrinkly.

Daddy takes over talking. "We didn't think the adoption would come through until next year. Then we got the call yesterday. And everything's happening so fast. We just wanted to be sure before we told you and got your hopes up."

"What about my puppy?" I ask.

Daddy scruffs up my hair. "Maybe we can talk about that one when we get back."

"When we get back from where?" I don't want to wait for my puppy.

"China," Mommy says.

"We're going to China?" I was on a flying airplane two times to see Different Granny and Gramps in California. You had to sit in your seat a very long time. What if China is as far away as California?

"Daddy and I will go there to get your new little brother, Nat," Mommy explains. "It's such a long flight. Granny will stay here with you. Won't that be fun?"

"You're going without me?" I am chokey in my neck now.

"You wouldn't want to miss your last week of kindergarten, would you, Nat?" Daddy asks. He has a fake smiley face on.

Tears are leaking out of me. Everything feels not fair. No puppy. No Mommy. No Daddy. No China. "Why can't I go with you?"

"We can barely afford two tickets to China, honey," Daddy says. "Besides, you love having Granny here."

"Not at nights." I have to swallow tears to get those words out. I love Granny. But Granny isn't Mommy and Daddy at night.

I don't eat very much for dinner. Neither do Mom and Dad. They both put me and Percy to bed early. It's still light outside.

"We have a lot to pray and be thankful for tonight, don't we?" Mom says. She sits on the feet part of my bed, next to Percy.

Daddy stays standing up.

They pray first. We say our regular prayers and make sure everybody we know is blessed, plus some people we don't even know.

Then Daddy says, "Father, thanks for blessing us with two children. Help them both know how much we love them."

Mom prays some regular stuff. Then she says, "Please keep our new baby safe. Give us a safe trip to China. Take care of Natalie and her granny while we're gone."

They're really much quiet. I know it's my turn. Only I don't want to tell God all the stuff in my head. So I just say, "Please bring my mom and dad back home super fast. Amen."

Mommy tucks me in and pets Percy's head. "You know, Nat, your dad and I will be back before you know it. And when we land, you'll have a brand-new baby brother."

A brand-new brother.

And no puppy.

Chapter 5

Sunday Showers Can't Grow Flowers

The next day is Sunday, and there is a lot of hurrying in our house. I'm late getting to my Sunday school room.

Soon as I walk in, Laurie waves at me from the front row. "Nat! I saved you a seat!" she yells.

My bestest friend, Laurie, is a great seat saver. I take that seat next to her.

"Tell me everything!" she whispers, on account of our teacher, Mrs. Palmer, is talking too. "What kind of a puppy? Do you get to pick? When will you—"

"No puppy," I whisper back.

"They changed their minds?" Laurie asks.

"I guess. We're getting a baby from China instead. A boy."

"You are?" Laurie is big in her eyes.

I nod.

"Wow! A brother!" Laurie says this so loud that Mrs. Palmer looks at us. Only she is smiley-faced like Laurie.

"I always wanted a brother," Laurie says.

"You did?" I'm surprised. Laurie acts even more excited about me getting a boy than she did about me getting a puppy.

Mrs. Palmer walks over to us. I think she's going to tell us to be quiet. Only I'm wrong. "Congratulations, Natalie," she says.

"Thank you." I'm pretty sure she means congratulations on the baby boy and not the puppy. I wonder if the whole world knows about it.

After church, Laurie and Laurie's mom run up to my mom when we're leaving. "Kelly, I can't find that pretty plate we used for the last potluck."

Mom stops walking. "Did you look under the sink?"

"It's not there." Laurie's mom looks aggravated.

"Are you sure, Marge? I put it right back where it always goes."

Laurie's mom shakes her head and takes Mom's arm. "You better find it. I'll need it before you get back."

"Go on, honey," Dad says. "I'll wait in the car." He walks out with Laurie's dad.

28

Laurie and I follow our moms down creaky stairs to the basement. There aren't good windows down there, and it's kinda dark.

"Why are the lights off?" Mom asks. She flips the light on at the bottom of the stairs.

"Surprise!"

"Surprise!"

"Surprise!"

A gazillion ladies shout this at us.

"I can't believe—how did you—I'm speechless!" Mommy says.

Laurie's mom leads my mom to a fancy table in front of everybody. Plus, there are presents on that table.

Laurie's big sister Sarah comes over to Laurie and me. "You guys can sit up front and watch," Sarah says. She puts us in the front row of chairs. "Have you ever been to a baby shower before, Natalie?"

"At Jason's house once," I answer. It wasn't so much fun. On account of there's no water in a baby shower. And the presents aren't for you.

"My mom was up all night planning this after your mom called," Sarah says. "Some people skipped church to go buy a gift, but don't tell Pastor." She laughs, 'cause you can tell our pastor all kinds of stuff.

"Nobody told *me*," Laurie complains.

"You can't keep a secret," Sarah says.

My mom keeps telling people thank you.

"Are you going to open your gifts or what?" Laurie's mom shouts at mine.

Everybody laughs.

Mommy starts to open a present, then stops. She looks right at me. "Natalie, could you help me open these gifts?"

I jump out of my seat and run up to her. I *love* to open gifts. I am a very good opener, that's what.

I start with the biggest present and pull off the bow. I rip off the paper. But the box is closed up. "It won't open," I tell Mom.

Together, we get it apart and pull out a big blue plastic thing. "It's a car seat," I mutter. I hate those things. Only the one I had didn't have toys on it like this one.

"It's amazing!" Mommy says. "Thank you so much. I really need it, too. We gave Nat's away. And this looks like a new, improved model."

I am already ripping open another present.

"Slow down, Nat," Mommy says.

Only I am a fast present-opener. I rip off the paper. "Diapers?" I push the giant bag of diapers away. This is the worst present I have ever unwrapped.

There are more worst presents. Rattles. And more diapers. Fuzzy blankets for babies. And little baby-boy clothes.

"You can finish," I tell my mom. On account of I am done opening these yucky-head presents.

Sarah lets Laurie and me pass out pieces of cake on little plates. But it's white cake and not chocolate. So I don't eat any. And I'm starving.

When the showering is finally over, Laurie's mom walks over to the basement steps, where Laurie and I are sitting. "Natalie, how'd you like to come home with Laurie?"

Most of the times, I would shout, *Yes!* Only not this time. Mommy and Daddy are going to China tomorrow. "I have to go home," I tell her.

"Please? We'd love to have you, Natalie," Laurie's mom says. "Your parents have a lot of packing to do. Let's give them some time, okay?"

"Come on, Nat!" Laurie says. "It'll be fun!"

We push through the crowd and get to my mom. I slip up and hug her. She puts one arm around me, while she keeps saying thank you to people. I don't think she'll want me to go to Laurie's. Sunday is family day at our house.

Mommy kisses my head. "Be good at Laurie's, Nat. Have fun."

I walk out with Laurie and Sarah. I take a fast look back before we step outside. I see other people and the pile of presents.

But I can't even see my mommy.

Chapter 6

The Truth about Brothers and Sisters

"*You* sit in back! I was here first." Brianna is Laurie's sister who's in fifth grade. She locks the front door of Laurie's van before Sarah can open it.

"You're there first because you didn't help us with the shower!" Sarah shouts.

"Please, Sarah," their mom begs, "just get in. You can have front both ways next time."

Sarah scoots into the backseat. Laurie and I scoot in after her. "Brianna always gets her way," Sarah mutters. She tosses a big Bible into the front seat. It lands on Brianna.

"Stop it!" Brianna shouts.

"It's *your* Bible!" Sarah shouts. "We're crowded back here."

Brianna tosses the Bible back to Sarah's lap.

Sarah tosses it back, hard.

"Mother, make her stop!" Brianna cries.

"Girls, please!" their mom shouts.

Brianna looks over the front seat at me. "See what you have to look forward to?"

"Me?" I get ready to catch a Bible.

"Yeah, you," Brianna says. "No more only child for you. I'd give anything to be an only child."

"If I'd had my way," Sarah says, "you would have been an only child … in someone else's family."

"Girls!" yells their mother.

"They don't mean it," Laurie whispers.

"Oh, yeah, we do mean it," Brianna insists. "You'll see." She turns on the car radio too loud for more talking.

At Laurie's house, we change into her clothes. She lets me wear her only purple shorts. We are the exactly same size, except she's bigger.

"I wish *we* were sisters," I tell Laurie.

"Yeah," she said. "Only maybe we'd fight like Sarah and Bri."

"No way!" I say, on account of Laurie and I *never* fight most of the time.

"Want to see what's on TV?" Laurie asks.

We go to the living room, but her dad has boring stuff on the TV. Like baseball. He's asleep in the big chair.

Sarah lies down on the couch. "Mother!" she shouts without opening her eyes. "Make Brianna turn her music down!"

It's true that Brianna's music is louder than the baseball noises on TV. Their dad is still sleeping through the whole thing.

Laurie's mom goes into Brianna's room, and the

music gets lower. Brianna sticks her head out of her door and screams, "I hate you, Sarah!"

"Goes double for me!" Sarah screams back.

"Let's go outside," Laurie says.

Instead of real swings, Laurie's dad hung a big tire on a tree. It's pretty cool. Only we both don't fit. Her tree isn't as big as Frank, the tree in my backyard. So it's harder to climb.

We sit by their sandbox. Only there's mostly dirt in there.

"What if I get a brother who's like Brianna?" I ask Laurie.

"Bri's okay," Laurie says. "I'm pretty sure she'll turn into a nice sister someday. Sarah did."

"Wasn't Sarah always nice?" I think Laurie's big sister is the prettiest and nicest sister I know. Plus, she wears lipstick. And once she painted my fingernails *and* my toenails.

"Sarah used to write 'kick' on my back and then kick me," Laurie says. "And she'd hit me without even writing first."

I can hardly believe this thing. "Really?"

"Really. Only she didn't kick or hit hard. And she always wrote with lipstick."

"Do Sarah and Brianna really hate each other?" I ask.

"Nah," Laurie answers. "They love each other."

"This isn't how we do love at our house," I say. "Are you sure?"

"Yep," Laurie answers. "Only sometimes they forget."

We go back to Laurie's room and have a picnic with her dolls. I'm a stuffed-animal girl, and she is a doll girl. Only we don't have to fight about it.

After our picnic, we walk out to the living room. Laurie's dad is still asleep in his chair.

"Shush!" Brianna says. She's kneeling by the couch, where Sarah is sleeping. Sarah is on her back, with one arm over her head and the other arm dangling off the couch.

"What's Brianna doing?" I whisper.

"I don't know," Laurie whispers back. "But that's Dad's shaving cream."

Brianna shushes us again.

We move in to see better. Brianna squirts a pile of white shaving cream into Sarah's dangling hand. Then she pulls out a feather and touches Sarah's nose with it.

Sarah's nose wrinkles. The feather touches it again. Sarah reaches up and scratches her nose. And that shaving cream goes all over her face.

"What?" Sarah sits up fast. White shaving stuff drips from her nose and chin.

Brianna is rolling on the floor laughing.

Sarah touches her nose, then stares at the white stuff in her hand. "You little—"

Brianna gets up and takes off running. "You're the one who did it!" she cries.

"And you're the one who's going to get it!" Sarah yells.

Laurie and her mom walk me home. Her mom talks most of the way about how happy I must be getting a little brother and not having to be an only child anymore.

I don't say anything. Only I'm thinking.

And what I'm thinking is how my mom and dad always say, "Only Natalie." Mostly they say this in a good way. Only sometimes not. And even then, I like being "Only Natalie."

Now I'm not going to be that anymore.

And I don't think I like being "Not-Only Natalie."

Chapter 7

Get Ready? Get Set? Don't Go!

Laurie and her mom walk me up my driveway. And that's when I see a strange thing. "How come Charlotte's here?"

"Charlotte?" Laurie's mom asks.

"That's her granny's car," Laurie explains.

The door opens, and there's my granny.

"Granny, why are you here?" My heart is very thumpy. "Where's my mom? Where's Daddy? Did they go to China?"

"Natalie, they would never leave without telling you, you silly thing." She hugs me, and I let her, on account of I think I need this hugging.

We tell Laurie and her mom good-bye. And thanks. Then we go on in.

"Your mom and dad are in the bedroom, packing," Granny explains. "I'm staying the night to help out."

I run into Mom and Dad's bedroom. Mom is opening and closing drawers. Daddy is reaching high up in the closet.

"Hey, Nat!" Daddy says. He takes a suitcase down from the top shelf. "Did you have fun at Laurie's?"

"Kinda."

Mom turns and gives me a smiley face. "Hi, honey." Then she goes back to her drawers.

"Can I help?" I ask.

"Sure," Mommy says. "Can you find me a handkerchief?"

"Yes!" I am a good helper. A really good helper. And this makes me have a thought. Maybe if I help enough, they'll take me with them.

Mom runs out of the bedroom, saying, "Gum! I better take gum for the airplane."

I pull open all the drawers and look very hard in them. But there aren't any hankies in here. So I dig more. And more.

Mom rushes back in. "Honey, please don't throw my things on the floor." She picks up the stuff that fell when I was looking.

"Here's a hankie," Daddy says, tossing it into the suitcase.

Granny comes in and asks if I want to play with

her. I go with her, but I don't feel like playing. So she helps me get ready for bed.

And Mommy and Daddy don't.

Granny reads me a story. And Mommy and Daddy don't.

Then Mommy and Daddy come in for the praying part. We all talk to God about taking care of Granny and me at home and Mommy and Daddy on the airplane and the baby boy in China. And that makes my heart feel a little better, only not so much.

In the morning, I don't feel like going to kindergarten. I stay sitting at the kitchen table when it's time to go. "I should stay here with Percy," I tell them.

Mom kisses my head. "Can't miss your last week of kindergarten, Nat. You be my big girl while we're gone. Okay?"

I don't feel like a big girl. I feel like it's the first day of kindergarten all over again. That's what.

Daddy bends

down to my size. "We'll miss you, Nat. But when we come home, we'll have a brand-new brother for you!"

I feel Granny's hand on my shoulder. "We better go, chum. Don't want to be late. Besides, Charlotte's been acting up again. That ol' Chevy is on its last legs."

I hug and kiss Mommy and Daddy more. And they do me more. Then I walk with Granny to Charlotte. Only I keep looking back and waving and getting waved at.

At school, Laurie and Jason are waiting for me by Ham the Hamster's cage.

"Nat!" Jason yells. "Ham wants his joke!"

Every day of kindergarten, almost, I tell our classroom pet a hamster joke. Only I don't feel jokey. Looking at Ham's cage makes me think about that mistake I made about the playpen.

"Come on, Nat!" Laurie shouts.

I join my bestest friends and look in at Ham. "Why did the hamster cross the road?" All of my hamster jokes start like that, sometimes. Then I have time to make up an answer.

"I don't know," Jason says. "Why did the hamster cross the road?"

"'Cause his mommy and daddy hamster flew in an airplane all the way to that other side of the road.

43

And that hamster didn't want to be left by himself. That's what."

Jason makes a frowny face. For the first time ever, he doesn't laugh at my hamster joke.

Me neither.

Chapter 8

Try, Try, Try Again

We have to take our seats. Laurie sits in front, next to Sasha. Sasha is not so nice. She and Peter the Not-So-Great are the two not-nicest kids in the whole kindergarten.

Anna turns around and whispers, "What's wrong, Natalie?"

There is so much sad in me. It must be leaking out. "My mom and dad are flying to China."

"China? Like the real China?" Anna pops out of her seat. "Cool! They should say hi to my great-grandmother!"

"I don't want them to say hi to anybody. I don't want them to go," I whisper.

"I've never been," Anna goes on. "But I want to." She gives me a frowny face. "It's really far away. Why are they going?"

"They're getting me a brother."

"No way!" Anna shouts.

"Stop talking, please," Miss Hines says. She's looking right at Anna and me. But she doesn't look aggravated. "Can you believe this is your last week of kindergarten? I'm going to miss each and every one of you. You better come by and visit next year."

This feels like one more sad thing to think about. Miss Hines is leaving me too.

"So," Miss Hines says, putting on her cheerleader voice. "Let's all share what we're looking forward to this summer. I'll start. This summer I'm going to be a painter. I'll be painting my house and my mother's house, inside and out."

"We're going on a really expensive vacation," Peter the Not-So-Great says without raising his hand.

"That sounds like fun," Miss Hines says. "Where are you going?"

"On a big boat!" Peter answers. "They put the whole Disneyland on there for my brothers and me. Goofy and Mickey Mouse and Batman will be there!"

"Wow!" Jason says. "Cool!"

"That's nice, Peter," Miss Hines says.

"Plus," Peter goes on, "it cost millions of dollars. But my dad doesn't even care."

"That's fine, Peter," Miss Hines says. "Anybody else?"

Sasha raises her hand, but she doesn't wait to get called on. Which is a waste of holding up your hand, if you ask me. "*I'm* going to Washington DC, our nation's capital."

"That's great, Sasha," our teacher says.

"I got to pick where to go for our vacation. And I chose an educational vacation. That means I'll be way ahead of other kids in school because I'll already know about presidents and the White House. We're not going on an old boat." Sasha makes a face at Peter. "*We're* flying on an airplane."

Anna raises her hand. But she looks at me when Miss Hines calls on her. "Natalie's going on a plane too. She's going farther than anybody. All the way to China!"

Miss Hines gets big in her eyes. She turns to me.

"Natalie! How wonderful for you!"

"No way!" Peter shouts. "You're lying, Natalie."

Everybody turns to look at me.

"Natalie, are you going to China? Is this true?"
Farah asks.

I shake my head in the no way.

"See! Told you so," Peter says.

Laurie jumps in. "But her mom and dad *are*
going on a plane all the way to China. And Nat
would go with them, except she doesn't want to
miss kindergarten."

Miss Hines looks like she doesn't know who
to believe. "Are they going to China on business,
Natalie?"

"Kinda," I answer. "They're picking up a baby
brother."

Miss Hines's mouth drops open. "Are they
adopting a baby from China?"

I nod.

"How wonderful! Natalie, you must be so
excited! When are they going?"

I look at the window and wonder the same thing.
"I don't know what time," I say.

"You mean they're flying to China *today*?"
Miss Hines is full of excited about this. "Well,
congratulations! Your news is by far the best. Right,
class?"

"Go, Nat!" Jason shouts.

I get a tiny bit smiley faced. Miss Hines is very smart. Plus, she wears glasses. And she says my news is better than anybody's.

"Class, aren't you excited for Natalie and her new little brother?" Miss Hines asks.

"Why?" Peter asks. "I have *two* brothers. My parents had Alex first, and he wasn't smart. So they had Michael, and he was too noisy. So they had me. It took them three tries to get me. But they did it! Peter the Great! Ta da!"

"*My* parents got it right the first time," Sasha says. "They would never ever have another baby."

"Now, Sasha," Miss Hines breaks in. "You don't know that."

"I do too!" Sasha shouts. "Why would they when they have me? They don't need another child. I'm enough for them."

Other kids talk about their sisters and brothers and summers. But I don't hear. On account of I can't get those Sasha words out of my ears: *"I'm enough for them."*

And I can't keep from wondering how come *I* wasn't enough for *my* parents.

Chapter 9

Stormy Brains

Kindergartners are more noisy than usual. In the afternoon, we sound like bumbly bees.

Bumbly bees make me think about airplanes. And that makes me wonder if my mom and dad are in one yet.

"Class!" Miss Hines shouts. "Please stop. I have an announcement."

Even this doesn't stop the bees.

"I'd hate to have us lose recess our last week of kindergarten," Miss Hines says.

That pretty much does it for the bumbly bees.

"Thank you. Now, first of all, I've only heard back from about half of your parents on the number of seats they'll need for graduation."

This is all new news to me.

"I don't get it," Jason says. "Why do *they* need seats for *our* graduation?"

"I sent a sign-up sheet home with you last week, Jason," Miss Hines says.

Jason is my bestest friend who is a boy. He's like me. We aren't very good with taking papers home. Jason loses his before it's time to go home. I make it home with mine. But I forget those papers are living

in my pack. On account of there are so many papers
in there.

"My parents are coming," Sasha says. "And
my grandparents and three aunts and two uncles. *I*
turned in *my* paper already."

"If you've turned in your paper, we don't need to
hear from you. Thank you," Miss Hines says.

"My parents are coming!" Peter says. "Only not
my two brothers because we can't trust them not to
make rude noises."

Other kids try to tell Miss Hines who's coming.
Only they all say it at the same time.

Farah raises her hand and waits for Miss Hines
to call on her. "Miss Hines, please, what is there to
see at this graduation?"

"Good question, Farah," Miss Hines says. "Our
kindergarten graduation will be Saturday morning.
One by one, you'll walk across the gym stage. And
you will get your graduation diploma. It's a piece of
paper that says you've finished kindergarten."

"Is that all?" Chase asks.

"As a matter of fact, it's not all." Miss Hines
grins like she knows a secret we don't. "We're
going to put on a little program for your parents."

"What kind of program?" Sasha demands.

"I'd like each of you to say a little piece," our
teacher says.

"A piece of what?" Jason asks.

Miss Hines gives us a huge smiley face. "That's up to you. I want you each to say something your moms and dads will like. I need your ideas. Remember how to brainstorm?"

We did brainstorming when we fixed up our classroom. Plus, we did it when Bethany broke her arm and we had to do something nice for her. Pretty much, we all talked at the same time. And instead of getting aggravated at us, Miss Hines just called it "brainstorming."

"I know what brainstorming is," Sasha says. "That's where we all shout out ideas. Only most of them are dumb." She turns and makes a frowny face at me.

"No such thing as a dumb idea in brainstorming," Miss Hines says. "Let's get started. Maybe you could say something nice about your parents."

"Like what?" Griff doesn't raise his hand. And this is okay in a brainstorm.

"Think," Miss Hines says. "Why do you need your mother?"

"She's the only one who knows where the Scotch tape is," Peter says.

"True. But let's keep thinking," Miss Hines says. "What do you suppose your mother was like when she was a little girl?"

"I don't know," Sasha says. "But my guess would be ... pretty bossy."

Miss Hines sighs and tries again. "What about your dads?" she asks the rest of us.

"My dad doesn't have any hair," Brooks says.

"*My* dad is king of the remote control!" Seth shouts.

"Hmm." Miss Hines looks like she might give up on our storming brains. "Let's try something else. What have you learned this year?"

"Not to run in the halls!" Jason shouts.

"I learned to read," Farah answers.

"Adding and subtracting," Anna says. She's a very good adder and subtracter.

I'm thinking this is a pretty good idea. I've learned a lot of stuff at kindergarten.

"Good!" Miss Hines exclaims. "Between now and Saturday, I'd like you to come up with the best thing you've learned all year. And Saturday morning, you can tell your family in our program."

I love to be on a stage and say things, on account of I might be a movie-star girl when I grow up. I picture me on the gym stage, with my mom and dad watching, all smiley faced at me, clapping their hands off.

Then that picture turns to horrible. I am on the stage, looking out at their smiley faces, but they're not there!

What if I say a piece and they don't hear me?

What if they are still in China with their brand-new kid?

Chapter 10

Trading Up

The second our class ends, I run out of my classroom. I have to catch Mom and Dad before they go to China and miss my whole entire kindergarten show.

"Nat! Wait up!" Laurie hollers.

I wave back to her. "I can't! I'll call you!" I walk superfast down the hallway.

I'm almost the first kid outside. I look for Charlotte the Chevrolet, Gran's car. Only I don't see that old car. *What if Charlotte broke again?*

"Nat! Over here!"

I race to my granny. "Granny, we have to go! Right now!"

"What's the rush?" Granny asks.

"Hurry! Hurry! Hurry!"

In my head, I see Daddy walking out of our house and yelling for Mom to hurry. I see them getting into their car and leaving. "Please, Granny!"

"All right. Keep your shirt on." Granny gets in the car, and I climb in the other side.

"So where are we headed in such an all-fired hurry?" Granny asks.

"Home!" I cry. "Or the airport. I have to catch Mom and Dad."

"Honey, they already left," Granny says.

"No! I don't want them to leave. Call them and tell them to come back!"

"They'll come back, honey," Granny says. "We'll pick them up at the airport on Sunday, right after church."

"That's too late!" I'm stuck now between sad and mad at them. They should be home. With me. Watching me on the stage in kindergarten. That's what.

"I know you miss them, Nat. But they're bringing you a brother. That's worth it, don't you think?" Granny waits for me to say yes.

Only I don't feel like saying yes.

I feel like saying no.

On account of I will be the only kid in the whole kindergarten not to have a mom or dad watching them graduate.

"Nat? Don't you notice anything different?" Granny asks. We're still sitting in the kindergarten parking lot. There is nothing different here. "Come on. Fasten your seat belt."

I reach for Charlotte's seat belt. Only something is very wrong. This isn't Charlotte's seat belt. I look around. The seat isn't torn. There's no gray tape on the glove box.

"Granny!" I cry. I reach for the door handle. "This is the wrong car!"

"Keep your seat, Nat," Granny says, grinning. "I traded up." She pats the steering wheel. It's black, instead of blue like Charlotte's.

"You what?"

"I finally got rid of that old car. How do you like my new one? Okay. Not exactly new. But still—"

"You got rid of Charlotte?" I cannot believe this thing. "Granny, you loved Charlotte the Chevrolet!"

"That's true," Granny admits. "But do you have any idea how many times that hunk of junk broke down on me last month alone?"

I know this is a true thing. On account of I was with Granny one time when Charlotte quit on us. Still, I feel sorry for her old car.

"Don't you like this newer car better?" Granny has proud all over her face. "I have air-conditioning again." She turns it on.

I put my face to the little blower on my side. The cold air feels great. But as soon as I think this, I feel like I'm a traitor to Charlotte. "I loved Charlotte," I say.

"And you'll love Charley too," Granny promises.

"Charley?"

"Charley the Chevy," Granny says. She pulls on her seat belt. "If I can just remember how this thing works ... There!" The belt snaps.

I buckle my seat belt. Granny backs out of her parking place. Cold air is still blowing inside the car. But I roll down my window like I did in Charlotte. Only in Charlotte, I had to really roll it. Plus, the window only went down halfway. Charley's window button works like in Laurie's van. All you do is push.

Laurie's mom is pulling out of a parking spot too. "Cool new car!" Laurie yells.

Laurie's right. This new car is very cool. Only I can't like it. I like Charlotte. And it feels like one more sad thing to have Charlotte be gone.

Granny backs Charley out of the parking spot. "This car drives like a dream, Nat. What a great trade-in I pulled off!"

I don't think Granny misses Charlotte at all.

And as we drive off, I wonder if my mommy and daddy miss me at all.

Chapter 11

Adopt-A-Pet

"We're going the wrong way, Granny!" I shout. Granny's new car is going up the hill. Not down the hill. "Charlotte would never go the wrong way home."

"That depends . . . ," Granny says. She takes another wrong turn. "On where you're going."

I don't care where we're going 'cause my mom and dad aren't anywhere anyway.

"Don't you like my new car, Nat?" Granny asks.

This new car doesn't bump hard across the railroad tracks. It doesn't squeak when Granny stops it. Plus, it has cold air. But I loved Charlotte. So I can't love Charley. "I miss Charlotte, Granny."

Granny drives past the ice-cream store. And the post office. She turns again, and Charley doesn't even screech.

"Where are we going?" I ask.

"You'll see," Granny answers. "It's a little surprise your mom and dad and I cooked up this morning."

"Really?" I'm surprised they cooked up this surprise. For me. Thinking about them making me a surprise takes a little of the sad away. "What's the surprise?"

"Want a clue?" Granny asks.

I remember those other clues. Like the string cage. And how I added up those clues and came out with a dog instead of a boy from China. "No thank you."

Granny turns into a driveway and stops. "We're here!"

I peek through Charley's window. I've seen this place before. But I was never in there. It's a big blue building with cats and dogs and animal footprints all over it. This is where Jason got his cat.

"How come we're here?" I ask. "I don't get it."

"But you're going to get it," Granny says. "That's a clue, in case you didn't notice."

"Granny, I'm no good at cl—" I stop. On account of my heart is getting thumpy about that clue. I'm going to get it? *It?* Here? At Adopt-A-Pet? I turn to ask Granny. Only I'm scared to think this thought again.

"Nat," Granny says, "how'd you like a puppy?"

"For true?" I ask. "Granny, a puppy?" I reach to hug her, but I'm stuck in my seat belt. It takes me a gazillion minutes to get it off 'cause it's not Charlotte's seat belt.

Granny has trouble with her seat belt too. "Your mom and dad thought a puppy might come in handy while they're in China."

"They were right about that!" I agree.

Granny and I run up the steps to Adopt-A-Pet. Only Granny walks. "Hold your horses, Nat!" she calls.

I look down three steps at Granny. "I'm going to hold my puppy. That's what!"

Inside, a lady is waiting for us. Her hair is almost as long as Farah's. "Can I help you?" she asks.

"We want a puppy!" I shout.

She laughs. "Well, you came to the right place."

Granny has to read papers and sign something. It takes a gazillion minutes. Finally, they get done.

"Follow me," the lady says. "What kind of dog are you looking for?"

"A puppy!" I answer.

"Size small," Granny adds.

The lady opens the door to another room, and barking comes out. Lots of barks. Inside, there are cages on top of cages. In each cage, there's a dog in there. It feels like a dog zoo.

"Look them over," the lady says.

I hold Granny's hand, and we walk along the cages. One dog is so big, he almost doesn't fit. Another fuzzy dog stays sleeping. More dogs bark when we walk by them. Black dogs. Brown dogs. White dogs. Long hair and no hair.

"Granny, how can I pick one?" I ask. "I want them all. Except maybe not that mean, growling one."

"I'll leave you to it," says the lady. "Back in a few."

Granny and I are alone with the gazillion dogs. "What if I pick the wrong dog?" I ask her.

Granny stares at the dogs too. "How about we pray that you'll know which is the right dog? Good idea?"

I nod. I close my eyes, but the barking sounds louder that way. So I open my eyes. I can tell Granny is waiting on me to do the praying.

I never prayed a pick-the-right-dog prayer before. So I have to guess how it goes. "God, which one's the right puppy for us? I'd really like to be sure about that one. Amen." I look up at Granny.

"Was that okay?"

"That was just right, Nat," Granny says. "You know, your mom and dad have been praying a prayer just like that one for a couple of years."

"They wanted a puppy?" I ask, surprised.

Gran chuckles. "No. They wanted a child."

Some of me wonders if they wanted a child as much as I want a puppy. The rest of me wonders why. "Why did they pray that, Granny? They already had me."

"Before they had you, Nat, your mom and dad prayed God would give them a baby. You were the answer to that prayer. And they thank God every day for you."

I know that's a for-true thing. "So why do they want another baby?"

"I think God gave them that *want*. And this time God chose to answer their prayers by letting them adopt a boy from China, a boy who really needs a home."

The door opens, and the lady comes back. "Made your pick yet?" she calls.

"Not quite yet!" Granny calls back.

I walk up to the cages again. A pointy-nose dog jumps up on the bars and scares me.

I peek in at a little brown dog with no hairs. "Here, boy!" I call. But he won't turn around.

A big red dog is panting in the next cage.

"I still don't know which dog to pick, Granny." Maybe I didn't pray hard enough.

A big puppy kind of dances in a bottom cage. It's brown, with floppy ears and hair that's not short and not long. I get down on my knees to see it better. The dog trots up and licks my hand through the cage bars.

"Granny, this one likes me!"

The Adopt-A-Pet lady walks closer to where we are.

The big brown puppy sticks out a paw. I think it wants to shake hands. Its foot is so big it makes me giggle. And just like that, I know this is the dog I'm supposed to pick. Like maybe that puppy prayer worked already.

"What kind of a dog is this one?" Granny asks.

The lady bends down and stares into the cage. "Your guess is as good as mine. But you don't want this one. Look at the size of those paws. That puppy's going to grow to be one giant dog."

"Ah. Better keep looking, Nat," Granny says. "I promised your folks I'd get a dog that would fit in the house."

"But—" Words won't get past the chokey in my neck. I want *this* puppy. This puppy picked *me*. And I picked her. And we picked each other.

And if I can't have this puppy, I don't want a puppy. That's what.

Chapter 12

Name That Puppy

"Come on, Nat," Granny says, moving to the next cage. "There are lots of cute dogs here."

"But I really want *this* puppy, Granny." Inside, I am telling this to God. On account of Granny listens to God more than to me. *Please make my granny want this dog.*

"On the plus side," the Adopt-A-Pet lady says, "this one's housebroken already."

Granny wheels around. "Housebroken? This big puppy is housebroken?"

"Only one here I'm sure of," the lady says.

Granny looks at the puppy, then looks at me. "Sold! Nat, you got yourself a puppy."

"Yippee!" I shout. The puppy shouts too. Only with barking.

The lady unlocks the cage and hands me my puppy. She's kinda heavy and squirmy, but I can carry her myself.

My puppy and I have to wait in the Adopt-A-Pet office so Granny can sign more papers. I whisper a big, fat thank you to God for the best dog in the whole world.

I wish Mommy and Daddy could see my puppy.

Granny walks out with a little cage. "Bought your dog a kennel," she says.

We load my puppy into the kennel. All the way home, I try to think up a name.

"What about Brownie?" Granny says.

"It's not special enough," I tell her. "And not Fido or Pickles or Jill or Mary Kay, either."

When we get to my house, I take my puppy out of the kennel. She tickles her wet nose against my neck. And I feel something inside of me that I'm pretty sure is love.

"I love my puppy, Granny."

"Looks like it goes both ways, Nat," Granny says.

I'm surprised that love can happen that fast. "I love you, Puppy 24," I whisper. That name just comes to me out of nowhere. "Granny, that's it! I'll call her Puppy 24!"

"Not bad," Granny says, scratching my puppy's floppy ear.

"We can call her Puppy for short." I am loving this new name. On account of I go by the name of Natalie 24. And my cat, Percy, goes by the name of Percy 24.

"Puppy 24," I say, while Granny and I walk to the house, "just wait until you meet Percy 24!"

"Yeah," Granny says really soft. "Just you wait."

Granny unlocks the front door, and Puppy and I race inside. "Percy! Percy! Where are you?"

Percy does not come running.

Percy never comes running unless it's his idea.

"I'll bet he's in my room," I tell Granny and Puppy. "That cat loves my room best of all." I love that about my cat. He could sleep anywhere in our whole entire house. But he picks out my bed. With me in it.

"Percy 24, have I got a surprise for you!" I carry Puppy to my room. And there is Percy curled up on my bed. "Found you!" I shout.

I scootch in next to Percy, with Puppy on my lap. "Percy 24, meet Puppy 24."

Puppy's tail wags so fast that it thumps my arm. She slides off my lap and tries to touch noses with Percy. They are exactly the same size. Except Puppy is bigger.

All of a sudden, Percy wakes up. He jumps to his feet. His white fur stands up on his sticking-up back. *Ffffft!* Percy hisses. *Yeowl!* Percy says.

"Percy!" I shout.

Percy hisses again. Then he jumps off my bed and runs out of my room.

Chapter 13

Percy 24 vs. Puppy 24

"Percy! Come back here!" I can't believe what my cat just did. "That's so not nice!" I call after him. "Bad cat!"

Puppy's tail stops wagging. She hides her head under my arm. She is shaking like a scaredy-cat.

Granny walks in. "I just met Percy in the hall. What did I miss?"

"Percy scared Puppy, Granny. Why would he spit and be so mean to my puppy?" I keep petting the soft brown fur.

Granny sits down with Puppy and me. "That cat of yours has ruled the roost around here for a long time. I suppose having another pet in the house will take some getting used to."

"But all Puppy wanted was to be friends," I tell her. I am very aggravated at Percy.

"Try hard to understand, okay, Nat?" Granny asks. "That cat has given you a lot of loving."

"I know," I admit. "Percy stayed with me when I was sick for almost a whole week."

"And remember how he let you and Laurie dress him up and push him around in Laurie's doll baby buggy?" Granny adds.

"Plus, he was my helper detective. Kind of."

"So give him some time to get used to the idea of another pet," Granny says. And I agree with her.

Granny and I have to go out and buy puppy food. Plus a puppy food dish. And a water dish. And a collar. And a leash. And puppy toys.

When we get back, Percy is sitting on our front step. I hold him while Granny opens the door. And guess what. Percy purrs.

Inside, I set down my cat. Then I run to free my puppy from the kennel.

Arf! Arf! Puppy jumps against her kennel. When I open it, she jumps on me.

I carry my puppy to the living room. "Percy?" I call.

But Percy already isn't there.

That night Granny and I put Puppy to bed in her kennel. Then Granny tucks me and Percy in.

"Granny, do you think Mom and Daddy will love Puppy 24?" I ask.

Granny sits on my bed between Percy and me. "I'm sure they will. Those two have a lot of love in them."

We say our prayers. Granny goes first. She prays for Mommy and Daddy and China. And for her new grandson.

Granny prays more stuff. Only I stop hearing after that word, *grandson*.

"Nat? Aren't you going to pray?" Granny asks me like she's been waiting forever.

I start out with "God bless everybody." Only I wonder if Mommy and Daddy are praying this right now too. Only in China. And my head is wondering if right now they are tucking in their other kid. And praying with *that* kid.

And I wish they were doing that with me.

Charley the Chevy takes me to school the next morning early. Plus, Granny lets Puppy come along for the ride. When we pull in, Jason is running circles around a bigger kid.

I open the car door and yell, "Jason!"

Jason waves and runs over to us. "Hey, Nat! What's up?"

I take Puppy out of the kennel and hold her up. "I have a dog! That's what!"

"Cool dog!" Jason shouts. "Is it coming to kindergarten?"

I make my eyes big at Granny. On account of I think Jason has a great idea.

Granny shakes her head.

"Nope," I answer Jason.

"See ya!" Jason runs off.

We wait until Laurie's mom drives up. She parks right next to us.

"Hi, Nat!" Laurie calls, getting out of their van. "Why didn't you call me last night?"

"I did!" I shout back. "Brianna said she'd tell you."

Brianna gets out of the backseat. "I'm not your answering service."

"Come and look, Laurie!" I cry.

Laurie runs over. "You got a puppy!" She makes

a squeaky noise like Charlotte the Chevrolet used to.

I let Laurie hold my puppy. Her tail whacks both of us in the face. "Her name in Puppy 24," I tell my bestest friend.

"I love that name!" Laurie says.

We both say good-bye to Puppy 24. And this is a hard thing. "Bye, Puppy!" we shout, walking backwards from the car to our school.

Granny shouts out the window, "Hey! What about me?"

"Bye, Granny!" I shout.

"You are so lucky!" Laurie says.

"I know!" Without closing my eyes, on account of I don't want to run into anything, I whisper a thank you to God for my puppy.

"A puppy and a little brother all in the same week!" Laurie says.

That stops all my happy from bubbling up.

We walk down the hall without talking. Only I have the feeling that God is still hanging around and waiting for me to whisper thank you again. Only this time for my little brother. So I kinda do. Only I don't really mean that one. And I know God knows it.

Chapter 14

Not So Fun with Math

Kindergarten is pretty much wild again. So we get to do more talking in class. By lunch, I've told everybody in my classroom that I got a puppy.

After lunch, we are even more filled with noise.

"Boys and girls!" poor Miss Hines shouts. "I know you're excited about graduating, but you're not out yet. We still have work to do."

She writes on the board. Then she spins around and shouts, "Time for fun with math!"

I never ever have fun with math.

"I'd like to have Laurie, Sasha, and Anna come up, please."

Their desks squeak. Laurie gives me a smiley face before she walks up.

"Good," says Miss Hines. "Now, Jason, Chase, Seth, and Brooks."

Those boys push and shove each other to get to the desk.

"Now," says Miss Hines, "which group has more?"

"*They* do," Sasha says, like she's mad about it.

"Right. How many boys?" Miss Hines asks.

"Four!" Peter shouts without raising his hand.

"And if we add our three girls?" Miss Hines asks.

"We've got seven," Sasha answers.

Our teacher writes on the board: "4 + 3 = 7." The boys elbow each other while her back faces them. They stop when she turns back around. "When we add two numbers, do we have more or less?"

"More!" we shout. On account of even I know adding gives you more. Adding isn't too bad. But subtracting is.

We add girls. And subtract girls. And add boys. And it's still not fun with math.

In the end, our teacher gives us a worksheet. Worksheets are very not fun. Miss Hines gives us time to do our work. Only I do more talking about Puppy to my friends than I do math. So I have to take my worksheet home to finish.

Granny tries even harder than our teacher to teach me math. We add up chocolate-chip cookies at the kitchen table. Then we subtract those cookies by eating them. But we run out before I finish my worksheet. Plus also, our tummies ache.

"How about this?" Granny jumps up from the table. "You and I and Puppy and Percy are in the kitchen, right?"

Puppy is sitting on my feet. I have to look around until I see that fluffy Percy curled up on the rug by the sink. "Yeah."

Granny acts like she's opening Christmas presents. "All right! That makes how many in the kitchen?"

"Four." I look at my math problem: $4 - 1 = ?$ I know that one already. Only Granny is having too much fun teaching me.

"We'll take away one." Granny runs out of the kitchen. "How many are left, Nat?" she shouts from the hallway.

"Three, Granny!" I shout back. I write the answer on my sheet.

That just leaves the bonus problem. I never do those. Sasha is the only one who does those when her parents help. And Anna can do some of them by herself. Not me. I fold my worksheet.

Granny comes back and sits next to me at the table. "Wait! We still have one problem left."

"That's okay. It's just an extra."

Granny unfolds my paper. "Nat, you can get this one!"

This one is: $3 - 2 + 3 = ?$

"It's too hard." My voice has whining in it.

"Nonsense." Granny points to the *3*. "How many people have you always had in your family, Nat?"

"Mommy, Daddy, and me." Saying this makes my neck a little chokey. I wish they were here now. "Three."

Granny points to the *2*. "Take away, or subtract, two of them as they fly to China, and that leaves … ?"

"One," I answer. 'Cause I know that's what Granny wants me to say. Only I am answering louder on the inside. *That leaves ME! That's what!* And my neck is getting chokier.

"Good!" Granny says. "So now we have one. And here come three more! Your mom and your dad and your new little brother. Now how many do you have in your family, Nat?"

I don't answer.

"Come on, Nat. You know this one," Granny says.

I do know this one.

"What's the answer, Nat?" Granny asks.

I don't want to answer. But my granny won't stop until I do. "Four," I say soft, writing down that answer.

"Right answer, Nat!" Granny shouts.

Only it doesn't feel like a right answer. And as soon as Granny walks away, I get out my worksheet, erase that 4, and write 3. On account of I don't like adding anymore.

Chapter 15

Last Days

Granny and I put Puppy to bed in her kennel. Only this time she doesn't want me to leave her. Somehow, this makes me sadder about Mommy and Daddy being gone.

I can hear Puppy whining when Granny and I go to my bedroom. Percy is already curled up on my bed. I curl up with him.

"Granny, I want them to be home." Tears leak out of me. "Why did they have to go get a baby? I liked it with just us. I don't need a little brother."

Granny sits on my bed and hugs me. Her cheek is against my cheek. She whispers in my ear, "Maybe God knew that your little brother needs you, Nat. He's so young. But he's already had a hard time in China."

"How come?" I ask, still staying hugged.

"He was born with his lips and mouth not quite right," Granny says. "That's why he got put in the orphanage."

I don't want to know this part. "Does his mouth hurt?"

"He's already had an operation on it. He might need more." Granny stops talking. I can feel that she loves her grandson already.

After more hugging, but no more talking, Granny says her prayers. I say mine. Then she tucks me in. When we're quiet, I can still hear my puppy doing whining in the kitchen. "Puppy's too lonely, Granny."

"I'll check on her, sweetheart." She pets Percy's fluffy back until he purrs.

"I wish Percy would like Puppy," I say. "Puppy just wants to be friends."

"You're right about that, Nat. Seems like that's how it should work, doesn't it? Percy's had a whole lot of loving his whole life. Puppy hasn't had much of it. She could sure use some of that love."

I get it. I know my granny is talking about more than cats and dogs.

In the morning, I run to the kitchen to see my puppy. She is already eating her breakfast.

"Natalie Elizabeth," Granny begins, "would you

like to explain this to me?" Granny never uses that "Elizabeth" name. Very much.

"What?" Then I see that she's dumped out my backpack. My graduation paper is on top of the pile. "It isn't important," I tell her. On account of I don't even want to go to that graduation.

"Are you kidding? You only graduate from kindergarten once, you know."

"I don't want to go," I say.

"Nat, do your mom and dad even know about this?"

I shrug up my shoulders. Inside, my answer is, *They don't care*.

Granny makes sure I have my math sheet. Plus also, she hands me the graduation sheet. "You turn this in. You hear me?"

I nod and stick it into my pack.

Kindergarten kids are wilder than ever. Poor Miss Hines gives up on doing work. We play games that are *real* fun, instead of *math* fun.

I almost forget to turn in my math worksheet.

"Good job," Miss Hines says when I give it to her. "What about your graduation paper, Natalie?"

I go back and get it. "Do I have to come if my parents don't?" I ask.

"I'm sorry your parents won't be back, Natalie," Miss Hines says. She takes another look at my graduation paper. "But it looks like somebody's coming to see you. You've requested three seats."

"Granny must have messed up marking that sheet," I guess. "Do I have to come?"

She puts her arm around me. "Well, I sure hope you do, Natalie. It just wouldn't be graduation day without you."

Miss Hines gives me a smiley face. And even though I don't feel smiley, I know that I am going to miss my teacher's smiley faces next year.

Granny acts very funny on my last day of kindergarten. When I wake up, she is making herself a toasted cheesy sandwich. On account of she's been awake so long that it should be her lunch.

Three times she drops stuff. A pan. Her shoe. Percy.

I wear my favorite purple shirt I drew on with markers. Granny lets me.

"Was that the phone, Nat?" Granny runs to the phone.

"No, Granny!" I call after her.

A gazillion times, she looks out the front window.

"Granny," I ask when she and Charley drop me off at kindergarten for the last time, "are you okay?"

"What?" she asks. Then she kisses my head. "Have fun at school, Nat. I'll pick you up. Deal?"

"Deal."

Miss Hines takes us one by one to work on our talking parts for graduation. I sit in the back of our class, so I am almost last.

Finally, she calls me to sit in the kid seat by her desk. "What are you going to say for the program tomorrow, Natalie?"

"I don't want to say anything. My parents won't be there."

"Well," Miss Hines says, "if you change your mind, I know you'll come up with something wonderful."

Laurie and I hold hands and walk out of our kindergarten class on the very last day.

"We really did it," Laurie says.

"Yep." I feel a little proud in my heart about this.

Laurie runs to her van. I look around until I see Granny walking up to meet me. "Hi, Granny!"

"Thought I'd never find a parking spot!" Granny calls. She has a huge smiley face on anyway. "Brought you a little surprise."

"Really?" Granny knows I love surprises. I'm already thinking of a gazillion surprises it could be. Like ice cream. Or a purple dress she'll make me wear to graduate. Or even Puppy 24.

I can see something in the backseat. Only the sun is too shining. I run toward Charley. Somebody gets out. And that somebody is my daddy.

"Daddy!" I scream. I run very hard to him.

Daddy picks me up and swings me over his head. Then he just hugs me. "Boy, did I miss you, Nat!"

I love hearing those words. "I missed you too!" I shout. Only it doesn't come out. On account my mouth is smooshed into my dad's shoulder. "Where's Mommy?" For a teeny second, I have a scary thought. What if she didn't come back? What if she's still in China? What if—"

"Nat!" Mommy steps out on the other side of Charley. "Honey, I'm over here!"

Daddy sets me down. I run to the other side of the car. "Mommy!" I scream.

She steps out of the backseat. I run to hug her. To be hugged up by her.

But her hands are full.

And they are full with a real, live baby.

Chapter 16

Runaways

I stare at the boy my mom is holding. He is wrapped in a green blanket. His eyes are black and look like Anna's. He has a lot of black hair. And I can see a scar on his lip, like the one Jason has on his arm.

"Are you sure it's a baby?" I ask. "Jason's baby was bald."

Mommy laughs. "He's almost six months old. But he's small for his age because he didn't get a very good start in life."

Part of me feels sad about that baby's bad start and the scar. Only the rest of me feels aggravated. On account of I want to hug my mommy, but her hands are full of baby.

"Want to hold your brother?" Mommy asks.

"No thank you," I answer. What I want to hold is Mommy.

Granny drives us home. I sit in front. They sit in back. We are two plus three.

Granny does all the talking. "Nat, I called your dad in China and told him about your graduation. I knew they'd find a way. And here they are. Now, isn't that something!"

"Yeah," I answer.

"I signed them up on that graduation sheet," Granny goes on. "So we're all set for tomorrow. Tell Nat what it was like the first time you saw Samuel."

"Samuel?" I ask.

"One of the nurses started calling him Samuel," Mommy explains. "The name stuck. I like it. Don't you, Nat?"

"It's okay," I answer. But it isn't okay. Well, it is. Only not all the way. There is no fanciness in that name.

"I'm still not sure about the name," Daddy admits. "*Samuel. Samuel*, go to your room. *Samuel*, stop coloring the wall. I don't know. It's like something's missing."

"Tell us about your puppy, Nat," Mom says, just when Granny pulls us into the driveway.

"Puppy 24 is a great puppy," I say. "Plus, she already loves me."

"How could she not?" Mom asks.

Granny and I get to our front door first. It takes Granny forever to unlock it.

"Hurry, Granny!" I can't wait for Mom and Dad to meet Puppy.

The door opens, and Puppy 24 comes running outside.

"How did you get out of your kennel?" I ask

88

Puppy. She lets me pick her up.

"I bet I forgot to put her in," Granny says. We walk inside. "I was in such a tizzy when your dad called me from the airport."

Daddy comes in and pets my puppy. "Pleased to meet you, Puppy 24." Then he takes the baby so

Mommy can hold Puppy.

"She's adorable," Mommy says. Puppy 24 wags her tail like crazy. I can tell she loves Mom already. "Will she grow any bigger?" Mom asks.

Granny laughs and disappears toward the kitchen. In a minute, she's back. "Where's Percy, Nat?"

I look around, but I don't see my cat. I hadn't even thought about him. "He's probably hiding."

"Why would he do that?" Daddy asks.

"He doesn't like Puppy," I explain. I check under the couch and in the big chair. I look out at the backyard. Then the front yard. My heart gets thumpy. "Percy!" I call.

"I hope I didn't let him out when I was in such a rush before," Granny says.

I run through the house, calling, "Percy! Percy!" Only he's not anywhere. What if he thought I didn't love him anymore? That I only loved Puppy?

When I get back to the living room, the baby is crying his head off. Granny, Mommy, and Daddy are in a circle around him. Making faces. Making goo-goo noises.

"Hey!" I cry. "Percy's gone!"

"He'll come back, honey," Daddy says. He jiggles the baby. But that baby keeps crying.

"No!" I can feel this bad twitchy in my heart. Percy's gone, and it's my fault. "Percy won't come back!"

"Nat, sweetheart," Granny says. "We'll all look for that cat together. Give us just a minute here. Okay?"

But I don't have just a minute. Percy ran away from home. And I'm the only one who cares. "Never mind!" I yell. I run up the hall.

"Nat?" Mom calls.

But I keep running. All the way to my room. On account of I am running away too.

Chapter 17

Adding It All Up

I can still hear Samuel crying all the way through my bedroom door. I am crying too. Only nobody cares about that.

Except for Puppy 24. She hops on my bed and licks up my face.

"Percy ran away, Puppy. He thinks I love you and not him. Only that's a lying thing. I love both of you!" I know this is for true. I know that adding Puppy made me love both of them more. "Adding means *more*!" I tell Puppy. "Not *less*!"

I put my face on Puppy's back and cry. Only inside I'm asking God, *Please bring my kitty back*.

Puppy squirms away. She hops off my bed and runs across my room. Her toenails *click, click*. She slips and bumps into my closet.

"Puppy! Come back!" I need her to be with me.

She doesn't come back. She keeps *scratch, scratch, scratching* at my closet.

My bedroom door opens. In come Mommy and Daddy and Granny.

"Nat, we're sorry," Mommy says. "Let's go look for Percy. Okay?"

I am crying very hard now. Mom sits next to me

and puts her arm around me. Daddy sits on the other side and puts his arm around me.

"Percy will be okay, Nat," Daddy says.

"I … love … Percy!" I say between cryings.

"Percy knows that," Daddy says.

"No he doesn't! He thinks I love him less 'cause of Puppy. But I love him *more*!" I feel arms tighten around me.

"Do you know *we* love *you* more than ever, Nat?" Mommy asks.

I don't answer. But I am doing very hard thinking.

"Now we get to love Nat the Daughter and Nat the Big Sister," Daddy says.

It feels good to be hugged on both sides of me. And I know I'm feeling that thing inside me that goes by the name of love.

"Sorry to interrupt," Granny says. "But why is that dog scratching up your closet?"

I slide off my bed and go to Puppy 24. "Come here, Puppy."

Puppy gives me a smiley face. Then she goes back to scratching.

Granny walks over to the closet. "I wonder …" She opens it just a crack. And out comes Percy.

"Percy! You're here!" I pull Percy onto my lap. "You didn't run away!"

Puppy's tail is wagging very fast. She tiptoes up to Percy. I wait for my cat to run out of the room like he did a gazillion times.

Only he doesn't. He stands up in my lap. But he doesn't spit. Puppy moves in closer. Percy holds very still. Then they touch noses.

"Well, I'll be," Granny says.

"They love each other!" I shout.

Percy prances off my lap. Then he strolls to my bed, jumps up, and curls into a curly ball.

I love that Percy.

Saturday, there is more hurrying in my house than on going-to-church days.

Granny drives us to school in Charley the Chevy. Mom and Dad and Samuel ride in the backseat together. Only it feels okay now.

We walk into the gym, and it is filled with noisiness. I help Mom and Dad and Granny get seats in the way back, in case Samuel turns into a crying baby. Then I go sit with my kindergarten class on our stage.

Laurie has a saved seat for me. "Is that your new baby brother?" she asks, full of excitement.

"Yep." I am a little full of excitement too. "You want to meet him after this?"

"Yeah! What's his name?" Laurie asks.

I start to answer. But Miss Hines walks to the

middle of stage, and everybody gets quiet.

"Welcome to our kindergarten graduation!" she shouts. People clap like crazy. Jason *whoops*. Miss Hines goes on to say a bunch of nice things about us. Then she asks her big question. "Class, what's the most important thing you learned this year?"

Katelyn has to go to the mike first. "Reading," she says. Then she sits down.

The next four kids copycat and say "reading" too.

When it's Jason's turn, he shouts, "I learned not to eat hot lunch on Fridays!"

Laurie goes after Jason. "I learned that it's okay to read at your own speed."

I think this is a great answer.

Farah smiles at Laurie and me before she goes to the mike. "I learned about friendship," she says.

Laurie and I cheer.

Peter says he learned he was "Peter-the-Even-Greater-Than-I-Thought-I-Was."

Sasha's answer is the longest: "I knew most of the things the other kids had to learn in kindergarten. So the best thing I learned was that I'm really good in math. And reading."

I'm still thinking up my answer when I hear Miss Hines call my name.

"Your turn!" Laurie says, pushing me to get up.

It feels like a long way to the mike. I peek into the crowd and see Granny. And Mommy and Daddy. And Samuel.

When I get to the middle of the stage, Miss Hines asks what she's asked every kid up here. "What did *you* learn this year?"

I don't answer. On account of I don't know what to say still. Chairs squeak behind me. Chairs squeak on the gym floor.

I know I should say something. Inside, I'm asking God what to say. Then the asking turns into thanking. *Thanks for kindergarten, God.* And I mean this. I liked kindergarten.

"Natalie?" Miss Hines says. "Can you tell us what you've learned?"

"I learned about adding," I begin.

"That's fine," Miss Hines says.

Only I'm not done yet. "I learned that I don't like subtracting much." Everybody in the gym is a little laughing. "But adding can be a very good thing in life. And I know this for true, on account of at my house, we just added my brother. That's what!"

Everybody claps. And claps even more. So I take a bow.

Miss Hines is laughing and clapping at the same time. "That's wonderful, Natalie. Want to tell us your brother's name?"

"Samuel," I answer. Only that name isn't fancy enough for my brother. I know that now. "Samuel 24."

We finish being graduated. I go back and sit next to Granny.

"I thought that name needed a little something," Granny says.

"Samuel 24 told me he wants his big sister to hold him," Mommy says.

"I'd like to," I say.

Mommy puts Samuel 24 in my lap. He fits. I give him a smiley face, and he gives me a smiley face back.

And guess what. I think I'm going to like being Not-Only-Natalie.